Gifts from Mexia:

My Small Alabama Hometown

Gwenyth Jaye McCorquodale

Parson's Porch Books
www.parsonsporchbooks.com

Gifts from Mexia: My Small Alabama Hometown

ISBN: Softcover 978-1-949888-10-2

Gifts from Mexia

Dedication

In Loving Memory of

Momma and Daddy

For

Bart and Beth

With Appreciation

To my husband Robin, who read each story so many times that he can recite each one. To those who served as cheerleaders—my sisters Ginger, Sherry, and Debbie—and to *The Monroe Journal* who published the articles I submitted and gave me confidence to write in this genre. To Steve Pitts, my brother-in-law, the black and white artwork in this collection awakens bright arrays of memories of time, place and the grace of my hometown. Every good story on paper has a great editor—thanks Becky.

Contents

A Letter from Gwen 11

Where Is Mexia? How Do You Say Mexia? 15

Gift One 21

A Pearl of Wisdom from Mother

Gift Two 25

Extravagant Abundance in Limited Conditions

Gift Three 31

Stop, Turn Around, and See the Other Person

Gift Four 37

Truths from the Ashes

Gift Five 42

Abundant Grace Found in Simple Gifts

Gift Six 47

A Birthday Treat and Birthday Wishes

Gift Seven 51

Life Can Limit the Body but Never the Spirit

Gift Eight 56

School Fears—Simply Smile and Trust

Gift Nine 61

A Teaching Legacy Shining Brightly

Gift Ten..66

Crazy Bad Things Can Be Crazy Good

Gift Eleven..73

A Mission Lesson in Memphis

Gift Twelve..78

A Song in the Air at Mexia

Gift Thirteen..84

Beauty Extends Beyond the Surface

Gift Fourteen...89

Uncle Click's Normandy Memories

Gift Fifteen..94

Gardens Remembered

A Letter from Gwen

Dear Reader,

In this collection of writings, I share snippets of my childhood experiences of growing up in the small, rural community of Mexia in Monroe County, Alabama, during the mid-1950s through the mid-1960s. The themes of family, faith, education, and community emerged as I compiled the writings into this edition.

My mother often told my sisters and me that the stories we read in books mirrored the real-life experiences of the people in our rural, isolated community. I'm not sure I believed her. How could rousing stories spring from people who farmed cotton and corn, and who attended Mexia Baptist Church at least three times every week?

However, as always…Mother was right. People in our community "walked through the valley of the shadow of death" and experienced the "joy that comes in the morning." Like generations before them, they had to wrestle with justice and mercy, decide between good and evil, find the power to forgive, learn how to control temptations, and accept or reject the goodness of God.

Mother's desire was for my sisters and me to travel and see the sights we read about in the many books she encouraged us to read. My sisters and I have been most fortunate to have travelled five of the seven continents and sailed four of the five oceans. We have toured major world cities and seen sights Mother dreamed of seeing. Daddy would wonder why we wanted to go in the first place! But the wonderful thing about Daddy is that he would be happy for us because our happiness was his happiness. No matter where we travelled or how far we roamed from Mexia, it is the home lessons we learned in our childhood hometown that linger closest to the heart.

These shared memories with my sisters—Ginger, Sherry, and Debbie—are central to these writings. As the oldest of the four girls—aka the "Jaye Girls"—I often tried to assume the know-it-all traits of the oldest child. It didn't work out so well. Ginger is far more sensible and responsible than I and has often been the guiding light to the family. Although I started piano lessons four years before Sherry, I have listened with pride as Sherry accompanied choirs and played at numerous events in south Alabama. Debbie, the last in line, had three older sisters who made her attend "their" school, and therefore, she is the best teacher ever!

Mother and Daddy encouraged educational opportunities, and when degrees were conferred on us, our greatest sadness was that Mother wasn't there. Ginger, Sherry, Debbie, and I had careers in education, between us teaching every grade from kindergarten to post-doctoral students. We believe that schools should be places of joy! We have also railed against practices and curriculum that rob children of this joy, and we have advocated for teachers to devote their gifts and develop their craft of teaching so that children discover the wonders of learning…it leads to joy for both the pupil and the teacher.

In these pages, I frequently speak from my perspective as an educator. I retired from teaching at Judson College where I served as Professor of Education, Head of the Department of Education, and Chair of the Social Science Division. My professional writings have been published by the National Association of English Teachers, the Association for Childhood Education International, the Reading Teacher, and other international and national journals. I coauthored the book, *Children's Fears of War and Terrorism: A Resource for Teachers and Parents,* also published by the Association for Childhood Education International. I served as editor of *ABC Strategies: Promoting Reading Success in the Content Areas*, a publication featuring summative coursework of teacher candidates I taught at Judson College. I frequently presented at international, national, state, and regional conferences about my research interests and about the importance of reading in a child's life.

As an antique shopper, I like to add to my collection of soup tureens, antique kitchen towels, and unique kitchen items. Civic work in Marion keeps me busy, as does writing for various civic publications. I often travel with my husband to markets in the US and Europe for furniture and gift items for his design business. Robin and I are the proud parents of Bart McCorquodale and Beth McCorquodale Lang, and parents-in-law to David Lang. We have two grandchildren—John Robin and Helen Clarice Lang—who are kind-hearted, and the apples of our eyes!

It has been a journey of reflecting on the gifts of my childhood as I've composed these writings. Some gifts are meant to be passed on! It is my hope that these lessons, which were gifts to me, will bless you in ways that enrich your spirit.

With best wishes,

Gwen

Where Is Mexia? How Do You Say Mexia?

Mexia Post Office

When I am asked, "Where is your hometown?" my answer can never be a simple one. After I reply, "Mexia, Alabama," a more detailed explanation is needed. I guess the unusual sound of the name Mexia seems to imply a foreign town, but my accent alone communicates a Deep South connection. Mexia is an unincorporated community in southwest Alabama in Monroe County about six miles from the county seat of Monroeville. Monroeville is known throughout the U.S. as the hometown of renowned author Harper Lee, and as the template for the fictional town of Maycomb in her beloved novel *To Kill a Mockingbird.*

On an Alabama map, Mexia lies about 1000 feet from the intersection of AL Highway 27 and the east-west US Highway 84, an important road in the early days of our country, for it connected Washington, D. C. to New Orleans. Generations of travelers have passed through Mexia on their way to larger towns.

Saying the name of Mexia correctly can be a challenge if you are not from Mexia. I was surprised to learn that Southern Living Travel includes it in their list of "Southern Towns You're Probably Mispronouncing" — not because the term doesn't deserve inclusion, but because no one ever travels to Mexia, Alabama.

Two towns in the United States bear the name of Mexia—Mexia, Texas, and Mexia, Alabama. True to the Spanish origin of the name, Lone Star state residents pronounce Mexia muh-HAY-uh. Residents of Monroe County, Alabama, pronounce it differently. A new minister to Mexia Baptist Church may pronounce it mex-SHU, but the sheep of his flock will quickly correct him with the God-given pronunciation of Mexia, which is MEX-ee. (The *a* is silent.)

My sister Debbie's friend from Atlanta came to Mexia to attend our mother's funeral. Not finding a landmark, she stopped at our uncle's store and asked a man sitting outside on a paint can if he could tell her where Mexia was. Impressed by her correct pronunciation of the area from someone bearing a Georgia tag, he said, "Lady, you're slap-right-up in the middle of it."

So, if you do not want to be stared at by the locals when you're in Mexia, Alabama, say MEX-ee…it rhymes with TEX-me.

Mexia, like most small, rural south Alabama areas, is steeped in a strong agricultural tradition. At the beginning of the last century, my grandparents eked out a living by farming. Just a few decades later, dramatic events at home and abroad changed even the small, rural town of Mexia.

When World War II ended, returning plowboys, like my father, came home from the fields of other lands to fields at home regulated by governmental agencies. Farming, like so many things in their lives, had changed; therefore, Mexia men found work in Monroe County at Vanity Fair Mills, or they became self-employed in construction or commercial jobs. Not surprisingly, after completing a full workday, these men came home in the late afternoon and early evening to feed small herds of cattle, plow cotton fields, and tend to family gardens of butter beans, peas, okra, tomatoes, and corn—the love of the land clung like the red clay on their boots.

In the mid-1950s, Mexia had, within 500-feet radius of each other, at least three businesses, a post office, a school, and three Protestant churches. Mexia Elementary School stood as the southern bookend of the community, and Mr. Julius Brown's general store anchored the northern end. If all students who attended the three-room schoolhouse in Mexia had perfect attendance for a six-weeks reporting period, Mr. Brown treated us to ice cream. Walking from the school to his store for the frozen sweet, we passed the post office that was painted sugar-white and a small clump of unpainted buildings with tin roofs that resembled those seen on the popular television show *Gunsmoke*. The back of Mexia Baptist Church was off to the left and Mexia United Methodist Church was on our right.

During the late 1950s and into the early '60s, the town of Mexia changed even more. The elementary school, two of the churches, the post office, and the businesses along the district strip closed or moved to different locations within the area of Mexia. Like Humpty Dumpty, the hometown of my childhood days will not be put back together again.

Mexia's rural, south Alabama location could be viewed by many as limiting. Perceptions and assumptions about rural communities, especially those of South Alabama, can be misleading. It was precisely Mexia's rural location that promoted family, faith, education, and community—factors that research studies praise for promoting healthy growth for all.

Our family network was wide and strong in Mexia. At church, a stained-glass window had my grandparents' name inscribed on it, which conveyed to me a heritage of faith. Most of my kinfolks lived either next door or within hollering distance from our house.

Mexia Baptist Church lessons stressed a personal relationship with the Father, Son, and Holy Spirit, the importance of a faith community, and a connection to something bigger and more important than self. My sisters and I missed the debut of the Beatles on the Ed Sullivan Show because we were at Mexia Baptist Church on Sunday nights reciting Bible verses and delivering Training Union messages.

I attended Mexia Elementary School for four years and understood that school and family should forge relationships that supported the community. My years in school at Mexia started me on a lifetime path that was enriched by learning and teaching.

Mexia's rural location positively contributed to developing a place of strong social traditions. Our house was in many ways a community house for Mexia: Mother hosted wedding showers, baby showers,

Women's Missionary Union meetings, and host of "singin's" on Friday nights.

In this collection of stories, I share lessons learned from people in Mexia—people who didn't know they were teaching me. These lessons from Mexia are gifts that unlikely teachers gave to me, and now I give them to you.

Mexia City Limit

A Pearl of Wisdom from Mother

Most can recall words of wisdom that their mothers gave to them as teenagers. However, my sisters and I don't recall Mother giving lectures on avoiding pitfalls that could suffocate the life out of you in your teenage years and beyond. That kind of advice could be found in the "Dear Abby" or "Ann Landers" columns in the *Mobile Register*.

However, we do recall a directive from Mother that took root so deeply in our collective psyche that it has become a pearl of wisdom to us. For over half a century, we have "applied" Mother's words every time we leave our houses: *Put on some lipstick!*

Mother expected big things from such a little tube. Hairspray, rouge, and even foundation were no match for a quick application of color from a tube of lipstick with a beautiful name like Pink Velvet, Sunset Orange, Brilliant Rose, or Ruby Red.

Like the magic wand used by Cinderella's fairy godmother, a good application of lipstick in the right color for your skin tone delivered a special magic. A dab on the lips could brighten the dullest complexion, highlight every hue of eye color, and give definition to the face. Of course, all these benefits made us feel like Cinderella.

I am still learning about the power of Mother's pearl of wisdom. Recently during two hospital stays at two different hospitals, I found Mother's advice to be transformational in helping me recover.

After I was taken to a Birmingham hospital by ambulance, a doctor, who is a friend, came to the hospital to evaluate my condition. Although I was in a semiconscious state, I remember him clearly saying to the nurse, *If I didn't know it was Gwen in that bed, I wouldn't recognize her. What has happened?* I tried to shout, "I don't really look that bad, I just need my lipstick!"

After the doctor left the room, I grabbed the nurse's hand and asked, "What time does Tom make morning rounds?" She replied that he usually made rounds around 6:00 a. m., which was only a few hours away.

I asked the nurse to hand me my purse. She assured me that I didn't need it, but I clutched her hand tightly and begged her to hand it to me. She acquiesced to my plea, placed it on the bed beside me, and I fumbled around until I found the treasure hidden at the bottom of the bag.

I didn't sleep much that night because I was waiting for 5:55 a. m. At precisely the "pumpkin" time, I smeared some Revlon lipstick on my lips. For my efforts, I was rewarded by the doctor's words, "You look much better this morning." (The noticeable improvement could not be credited to the intravenous medicines or receiving oxygen during the wee hours of the morning; it was clearly the effect of Pink Rose on the lips!)

About six weeks later, I went to Goat Hill in Montgomery to attend a campaign victory celebration, and just like Jack and Jill who went up the hill, I fell (I wonder if 500 people saw them tumble?) and sustained terrible injuries.

In the ambulance, the paramedics were completing an inventory of items to place in the vault at the hospital. Thank goodness, I had presence of mind to ask for my purse, and I quickly grabbed a tube of lipstick from the depths of the bag.

During my seven-day stay at the Montgomery hospital, I religiously applied long-lasting lip color at 12-hour intervals. The nursing staff noticed this bit of color on my face because at one of the 3:00 a.m. medicine rounds a nurse asked, "Honey, your lipstick has faded a little, would you like for me to hand it to you?"

So I survived some difficult days by simply adhering to Mother's advice: Put on some lipstick!"

Maybe Mother knew what research studies from the American Psychological Society confirm: Your health is better when you feel more attractive.

My sisters and I always knew we had a smart mother—Daddy told us so!

Extravagant Abundance in Limited Conditions

Mother's fascination with obtaining a Winnebago or an Airstream Excella was far removed from any outdoor adventure or any thought of pulling into a campground. Mother thought of a camper as a large, luxurious living room on wheels—a place where her family could be together to talk and visit—while cruising America's highways with ease.

Mother's vision of a happy family traveling in a recreational vehicle led to an outlandish idea, and her smart, college-educated daughters fell for it hook, line, and sinker.

The blueprint began to be drawn in Mother's mind as she planned a family Christmas trip to Richmond, Virginia, to visit our sister Ginger and her family.

On the day of our departure, Mother innocently commented to us, "There's no reason for us to take two cars. The hassle of following each other in that horrible traffic in Atlanta and Charlotte is not necessary. If we go together, we can talk and visit."

This was the reasoning as we planned our journey up the Eastern coast together in December of 1982.

If Mother thought an idea was a doable thing, and if my sisters and I agreed with her, Daddy's reasoning abilities were doomed to fail. One of my uncles commented in my presence that Daddy was hen-pecked. Out of respect for my elderly uncle, I held my tongue, but I silently shouted, "Try reasoning with five hormonal women and see who wins."

Well, Mother got her way about the camper, with some *major* alterations.

Neither minivans nor today's large vehicles that hold more than six passengers had rolled off the assembly lines in Detroit in 1982, so we thought that Mother meant we would rent a camper. However, this was never her intent.

Mother had designed a plan and we were fated to follow it: We would travel together in the cargo bed of Daddy's truck, which had a camper top! That's right! *Daddy's work truck with its CAMPER TOP!*

Sounding like a camper top salesperson, Mother started rattling off the advantages of Daddy's camper top. It was custom designed for safety, had a front window so we could tell Daddy how to drive and when to stop, and had an insulated roof and sides for noise control.

However, Mother got our attention when she noted that the children could roam around and play games as we travelled. This was music to our ears. It would have been difficult to keep four small children entertained for the ten-plus hours of riding.

However, Mother's main selling point came next. Sounding as if she were quoting Holy Scriptures, Mother ended her appeal by saying: "You know that a family who travels together stays together!"

On a cold December morning, Daddy, Mother, Debbie, Sherry, four children, and I started the 700-mile trip to Richmond in a Dodge truck with a camper top covering the cargo-bed. We lined the bottom of the truck bed with quilts and blankets.

Our first stop was for lunch at a fast food restaurant. I think Daddy stayed (hid) in the truck until we were inside ordering our food. Imagine the sight: Four women wearing full-length mink coats stepping gingerly from the back of the truck as four children escaped its confines and ran like a football team across the parking lot!

Oh, the stares and looks that silently said, "Alabama hillbillies are in town," and/or "Surely there's a movie crew filming a present-day 'Grapes of Wrath' movie."

After eating and sipping hot chocolate, we started the herding process of getting everyone back into our pretend Winnebago. As Daddy swung the children into the back of the truck, my sisters and I bombarded him with this order: Drive to the back of a gas station and we can exit the truck there. (We didn't want the scrutiny of the unappreciated glares of those who didn't know the advantages of traveling together.)

Thank goodness we arrived at Ginger's after dark, because her neighbors might revive any dormant suspicions they may have possessed about Alabama rednecks. To Ginger's credit, she didn't seem the least bit surprised as we piled out of the truck onto her lawn.

Our visit inspired Ginger to host a lovely tea to introduce her mother and sisters to neighbors and friends. Decorations that said, "It's Christmas Time" adorned the dining room table. Silver trays gleamed in the light of the crystal chandelier. Even the smell of cinnamon and spices enhanced the festive mood.

I was pouring punch as everyone gathered around the table to get finger sandwiches and Christmas candy when a neighbor said, "Since your cars weren't in the driveway, I thought you were delayed. In fact, where are your cars?"

I immediately lost control of the punch ladle and my thoughts swirled faster than the sherbet in the bowl as

I considered how to answer her, but Mother rescued me. She quickly replied, "Why, we traveled together. My husband has taken the children to the skating rink while we are enjoying visiting with you." (Boy, I admired Mother's ability to think so quickly and make our mode of travel not the topic.)

After a couple of days of visiting, we began to retrace our path back to Alabama. As we loaded into the camper, heavy snowflakes began to blanket the ground. Only eyes above the blankets and coats could be seen in the back of the camper as we traveled south on the I-85 route home.

At lunchtime, we stopped at a Shoney's Restaurant. Regrettably, Mother fell on ice at the entrance door and hurt her foot. All the way home, Mother's foot was throbbing, and we suspected it was broken. Four children and three daughters took turns rubbing the foot, as Mother refused to stop at a hospital.

In Birmingham, an orthopedic surgeon confirmed our diagnosis and explained that he could operate and set the ankle because the swelling was under control.

Before surgery the doctor said, "Mrs. Jaye, how did you manage to keep your foot elevated in a car for such a long distance?" Without missing a beat, as though she had anticipated the question, she said, "Well, I was able to stay flat on my back and keep the foot elevated above my head in our spacious traveling accommodations."

Mother was a paragon in understanding that extravagant abundance can abide in limited conditions. Oh, how the world could use her vision of life now!

The Richmond Christmas trip was the last family trip with Mother because she died suddenly the following July. My sisters and I know that it is a blessing to have had a Mother who wanted us to be together. We have continued the tradition by having "sister trips" each year.

Our Richmond family trip will always be remembered as a time when heaven's joy was present in a most unlikely place—Mother's makeshift camper.

Stop, Turn Around, and See the Other Person

The vintage Sunbeam Model S-4D iron displayed in the window of the antique mall caught my attention because it looked brand new—as if it had never been used. I thought how Mother and Olivia, a woman who helped Mother with the laundry, had put this model to the test at our house in the 1950s. As I looked at the old domestic device, threads of childhood memories related to laundry unfolded.

Mother approached all work as a learning time for my sisters and me, and under her tutelage we received scholarly instruction on weekday household chores. Following the pattern of the children's traditional folk song, Mother established a firm routine for us.

This is the way we wash our clothes,
Wash our clothes, wash our clothes,
This is the way we wash our clothes,
So early Monday morning.

Our Monday morning duty was to hang the washed clothes on the clothesline to dry. We hung sheets on the first line. Wooden clothes pin clamped bath towels and washcloths to the second line. Then, hidden from view of travelers on busy US Highway 84, we placed on the third line personal items like panties and bras.

Our wash looked pretty on the lines because we even sorted items by size and color. And Mother was right—we learned organizational skills from the work.

Tuesday's work matched the lyrics of the playful tune, too:

> *This is the way we iron our clothes,*
> *Iron our clothes, iron our clothes,*
> *This is the way we iron our clothes,*
> *So early Tuesday morning.*

Even if you didn't have a calendar to tell you it was Tuesday, the smell of starch and steam in the den told you that Olivia was at our house, busy at work. It was at least 30 degrees hotter in the den than any other room when the ironing board was unfolded.

Olivia didn't trust the bright red steam button on the new Model S-4D gadget, so she insisted that my sisters and I use a Coke bottle with a tin sprinkler head attached to the top to wet the clothes. Then Olivia rolled them in a tight bundle that resembled a cocoon—the clothes had no chance of getting dry. When Olivia's hot iron hit the damp clothes, a vapor so dense formed that it hid Olivia's black face.

Ironing was a chore that took all day for Olivia. Maybe someone else could have finished the task more quickly, but Olivia pressed the underside and the outside of every piece of clothing, including Daddy's underwear, household items like sheets, pillowcases, and even flour sack dish towels. A napkin received the same careful attention and care as Daddy's dress shirts.

When Olivia ironed your clothes, a linen blouse could be worn several times and it would remain stiff and crisp until the next wash day. I often thought that Daddy must have found bending down to lay bricks in pants starched and ironed by Olivia as hard as the cement he put between the bricks.

Mother noticed and appreciated the precise care Olivia took with the clothing, but she also said that Olivia liked to watch *The Guiding Light.* Mother even pointed out that the new electric model S-4D made Olivia's mundane job a little easier. However, after Olivia's death, mother emulated Olivia's ironing habits as she watched her soap opera. Many years later my mother-in-law couldn't believe her eyes when she saw mother ironing our new baby boy's diapers. I just said, "Oh, it's a habit she got from Olivia."

Taking Olivia home, after a tiring day of work for her, was a fun time for us. My sisters and I would jump in the car to go with Daddy. We loved rolling down the windows in the car and smelling the fresh scent of the trees and bushes that lined the long dirt road leading to Olivia's house. The shoulders of the road stood up from the leveled dirt road and the ditches were steep on the sides, very different from busy US Highway 84. If it was dry, thick red dirt from the back tires billowed as thick as the white poison falling on the cotton fields from Jennings Carter's crop duster plane.

However, when we got to Olivia's house, a troubling mood would settle over me. The wooden house looked as old and worn as the dirt in the front yard. A black iron wash pot with firewood crossed and blazing under it stood in the front yard, which made it look like a witch's cauldron. Olivia's daughter stood stirring the clothes in the pot with a long-handled stick.

On our way home from Olivia's, I asked Daddy about the washing pot and he told me that Olivia "took in" washing for several people. I began to think that ironing all day was easier than standing and stirring clothes in that boiling pot, until I realized that Olivia had to complete other jobs after work at our house.

As I was quietly pondering Olivia's life, my train of thought was interrupted by a chicken that appeared from out of nowhere. I watched in disbelief as the fowl suddenly became airborne and took flight right into the path of the car. The next sound I heard was a loud THUD!

Daddy bolted from the car to see about the chicken, but I knew he'd find a dead bird. I tried to calm my little sisters who were crying by saying, "Well, I guess we'll have fried chicken tonight." Daddy, who was slow to scold, gave me a look that meant this wasn't going to happen.

After Daddy retrieved the bird, he put the car in reverse and maneuvered it on the narrow road without going into the ditch. To my amazement we were stopping at every house along the dirt road to find the owner of the chicken. (Does a chicken have distinctive features?) For at least four stops, Daddy's inquiries were met with "No, it's not my chicken." Finally, we were back at Olivia's, who identified the fowl corpse as hers. Daddy dug in his starched pants and made sure Olivia was paid for the loss of her "laying hen."

As we left Olivia's house, I felt proud that Daddy had compensated Olivia. I thought of the Pharisees of old and how they'd reason and say, "accidents happen" and continue on their way without finding the owner. However, they would have missed many lessons related to the "Kingdom of God on earth." There is another way to travel life's road. Like the compassionate Samaritan, we often have to stop, turn around, and see the other person.

It is surprising how an object from the past, something as simple as an iron, can help you recall powerful lessons on topics that may seem new, but in actuality are age-old human issues: economic disparity, justice, racial harmony, and the Golden Rule—Do unto others as you would have them do unto you.

Truths from the Ashes

During the mid-1950s and into the early '60s, my sisters and I got pretty good at praying for miracles. We would deliver our petitions right on schedule, every Sunday night during family prayer time. Cocooned in my space on the covers of mother and daddy's bed, I'd reverently listen to my younger sisters run down the list of everybody (and almost everything) in the world for which they were thankful. At the close of each prayer, Ginger, Sherry, and I would send up the big one for our sister: *God, please let Debbie wear a size 6 shoe when she gets older.*

In our young minds, this was right up there with any revival preacher's fervent prayer. We prayed this because we wore size 4 shoes, and every fashionable and up-to-date preteen shoe started at size 6. Sadly, we wore "little girl" footwear—a fate that we didn't want for Debbie.

God surely had much more mighty works to perform, but He didn't shrug this one off. Debbie's feet grew to that size 6, and in her trendy high-heeled shoes, she looked prettier than the new Barbie Doll that had just arrived on shelves.

Although the prayer was an innocent and childish plea, we never forgot it. Over the years, it provided a framework for understanding some of life's big questions: Is God really there? Do habits of faith always produce good results? Can we depend on God to be with us?

In happy times, it filled our hearts with thankfulness. In times of despair and need, it called us to trust in the truths of faith we had learned as children. This was especially true when our mother died suddenly of a stroke at the young age of fifty-six.

Mother was far too young to die, and we were too young to be motherless. Our hearts were bruised and broken. After that, every step through the shadow of the valley of death felt less like walking and more like plodding. We were just putting one foot in front of the other.

Daddy tried to fill the void by being a mother to us. He buried himself in doing things she had always done. The man who had never opened a can was now canning pear, blackberry, and fig preserves. The same person who didn't know how to turn on the oven was serving up hot biscuits when we came home. He hated small talk, but suddenly he was a chatterbox, calling each of us every Saturday morning.

Visiting home after mother's death was like entering a shrine to her. Daddy's devotion to keeping things normal made it seem as if mother had just left the house to run a quick errand.

This changed on the morning of the coldest January 3 ever recorded in Alabama. Exactly six months after mother's death, an electrical fire consumed our house.

I reached Mexia from my home in Macon, Georgia, by early nightfall, just as the firefighters were leaving. They'd come from three different stations in the county, but only a burned shell of our house remained.

Debbie's husband Steve assured me that all was not lost for Daddy. He had peered through holes where windows once were and had seen that a few things still stood. Our beloved piano, which had been the center of many family memories, was in place, he said. A wicker chest that held our family pictures still supported a lamp.

Surely, there were other things.

Just as they had done six months earlier, family, friends, and at least half of the population of Mexia rushed in to surround us and offer comfort that night. Blankets, coats, scarves, and hats appeared as if pulled from a magician's hat, and warm, nourishing casseroles were delivered to our aunts' and uncles' homes—that's what Baptists do.

Then sometime in the morning hours that followed, my aunt awakened me. The fire had rekindled. I dressed quickly and hurried over. Fiery debris flew as firefighters once again tried to control the flames.

As I opened the door of the car, I watched as three of the outer walls of the house collapsed in the new blaze. But the fourth wall—a beautiful stone wall daddy had built—stood defiant, like a spire reaching upward toward the heavens.

The roof moaned as it slowly made its way through space to the floor. I can still hear the eerie plinks from our beloved piano when the roof finally crashed around it.

Surely, every memento, trinket, and tangible evidence of mother's presence was gone, extinguished.

But when I walked to where a group of men had gathered, I saw Steve and Daddy pulling a box from the ashes. There, lit up by the incandescent rays beams of flashlights, sat the wicker chest.

One of the men said to Daddy, "It's just hard to believe this survived." Indeed, it was virtually unimaginable. There, unharmed by the fire and unmarred by the relentless hose water, was that flimsy wicker chest. The stones and mortar of the fireplace wall had protected it.

We knew what it held: family pictures, certificates, high school yearbooks, and more. Speechless and in wonder of it all, we were filled with joy—a derisory word to describe the emotion we felt.

Joy, not because what was lost was found, but because of what was present and real that night and on so many nights that followed. A faith community supports your journey in life. A father's example of compassion and love can abundantly bless you. Hope, joy, and love can be found in the rubble and ashes of life.

Or is it more like this? In the rubble and ashes, hope, joy, and love find fertile soil to spring up and grow again!

Abundant Grace Found in Simple Gifts

Every time my sisters and I left our yard on our bicycles to go Uncle Glynn's store, we'd hear our mother's familiar warning, "Watch out for Henry Cranford." In fact, Mother used this phrase more often than "Eat your vegetables." Mother could and should have warned us about the clear and present danger of peddling our bikes on busy US Highway 84.

As enticing as the apple was to Eve, the shiny, black asphalt of this federal highway invited us to steer our bikes from the rough, dirt shoulders beside the road onto its smooth blacktop. We couldn't resist the lure of easy peddling even though dump trucks, log trucks, and 18-wheelers ran full-throttle ahead on this busy road. So we'd yo-yo on and off the velvety pavement.

If Mother ever worried about seeing the imprint of our bicycles smashed like dead bugs to the front of these vehicles, she never let on.

No, Mother had a fierce foe that rivaled all others: Henry Cranford. Mother had conjured up horrific horror scenes in her mind of the mayhem Henry could inflict behind the wheel of his souped-up V-8 engine car. Consequently, heavy and oversized road vehicles became lame and tame road adversaries compared to Henry.

Mother even made us practice a drill of our course of action if we heard Henry's car coming. (We could always hear the car before we saw it, for Henry revved the powerful motor—making enough noise to wake the dead.)

Mother's drill directions rang clearly in our heads: "Steer immediately for the ditch, drop the bicycles, and walk in the ditch to the store or back home." We dutifully obeyed every word because Mother had a fly-swatter that she used for "classical conditioning" purposes.

My sisters and I just knew that Henry spied on us, and that he purposefully left his house as we raised our kickstands. We never escaped the yard on our bicycles without hearing mother's recurring warning or the all-too-familiar roar of Henry's car.

The course of action was ingrained in us: We'd give up the right-of-way to Henry and steer, drop, and walk.

After gathering our bikes from the ditch, we'd swear that Henry had a smile on his face as he zoomed by. Infuriating humiliation!

My sisters and I never met Henry. Neither he nor his family attended Mexia Baptist Church or other community activities, which was unusual in our small, rural community. We were, however, intrigued by the fact that Mother seemed to know so much about him.

Mimicking Nancy Drew and Trixie Belden, my sisters and I eavesdropped on hushed conversations between Mother and Grandmother, and we surmised that Henry had been caught "boot-legging." We were totally confused. How did mother know Henry wore boots? He was always sitting in his car!

But there was more for us to ponder about Henry. If we were puzzled by Mother's warnings, we were even more sensitive to Daddy's actions.

On lazy summer Sunday afternoons, Daddy would take us down to the creek to play. Along our walk there, we'd stop to visit with Mrs. Gaines, Grandmother Jaye, Aunt Nona, and others who lived along the unpaved road to the creek. We'd also pass Henry's house, but we never went in the yard to visit.

In the deep recesses of our minds, we sensed that Daddy was protecting us from something we couldn't understand at our ages. Although Daddy said that Henry was a likeable, jolly man, we imagined scenes of all sorts of danger and darkness lurking in his house.

Years passed and bicycles were put away as we became young drivers. It was during these years that a phone call awoke us late on a Saturday night. A phone ringing at that time of night meant something was terribly wrong. Even though he wasn't a doctor or policeman, everyone called my dad whenever something unusual happened. After Daddy had quickly left the house, mother told us Henry's older brother had shot and killed Henry. Later we learned that the two brothers had engaged in a heated argument that resulted in the accidental tragedy.

There was danger and darkness just down the road, and I didn't understand then and don't understand now.

Henry did no harm to my sisters and me. I'm certain he did laugh at us, and I hope it was a good ole belly laugh. What a spectacle we must have made steering for the ditch!

More of the story…

Decades later on a sunny, bright day that was too cruel for our wounded hearts, we buried our mother, who had unexpectedly died from a stroke at far too young an age. Food was piled high on every counter in the kitchen and on the dining room table, as church and community came to comfort us.

A slight rapping at the back door drew my attention away from the group eating in the dining room. There stood a woman I had never met, cradling fresh ears of corn in her apron. Refusing to come in, she quickly gave me the corn and left. The absence of a car in the driveway told me that the woman had walked to our house.

In the kitchen, I asked Aunt Rachel about the woman, and she told me it was Henry's mother, who still lived on the old home place taking care of Henry's younger, invalid brother.

In the middle of sadness and grief, this simple gift of corn from Henry's mother led me to see the invisible presence of extravagant abundance in our house that terrible day.

Mrs. Cranford had travelled the same dark roads we were travelling. In truth, life can be bleak and dark at times. However, doing ordinary things that neighbors do to show compassion and care can create significant moments of grace. Mrs. Cranford surely did this for me!

A Birthday Treat and Birthday Wishes

With a milestone birthday approaching and my natural aging signs accelerating at an unnatural rate, I decided to do something less dramatic than surgical and cosmetic interventions to improve my physical appearance: I booked an appointment in Atlanta at a hair salon for a new hairdo.

I was even more excited to learn that the salon where a new and improved me would emerge happened to be the same one Julia Roberts and Jennifer Aniston frequent. Even gorgeous movie stars, who are masterful at creating the illusion, know that beautiful hair is not effortless; it requires a lot of attention and work.

While on the way to the salon, I was stuck in nightmarish traffic—so common to Atlanta commuters and so utterly mind-boggling to small-town visitors. As I drove, my mind wandered to childhood days and Mother's "beauty shop" in the kitchen and den of our house, where the pursuit of beautiful hair was a miserable and dreadful experience.

Just before suppertime on any given Saturday afternoon, screams seeped through the brick and plaster walls of our kitchen as mother laid one of my sisters or me on the kitchen counter and started spraying either too hot or too cold water on our tender, sensitive heads.

With the sprayer back in its socket, Mother commenced with squirting Joy dishwashing detergent to wash (never to be referred to as shampooing) our hair—Mother wanted that "squeaky clean sound" advertisers promised.

Then the scrubbing began. Mother accomplished this task with the same energy she devoted to scouring a scorched pan with Ajax. We were helpless little lambs, lying there with our eyes looking heavenward for help.

After towel drying, we little lambs sat at Mother's feet as she pulled the tiniest-toothed comb through our thick, tangled hair. As our harrowing screams erupted, Mother took strips of thin paper and started rolling strands of hair around into a tight circle and secured each with a bobby-pin that stabbed into the flesh of our already red scalps. Oh, what pain we had to bear!

Mother repeated this scenario four times every Saturday afternoon—once for each sister—and our overreactions would have defeated most mothers. But not our Mother! She was determined that curls would frame our faces. Angels had curls, and Mother was aiming for that appearance for Sunday morning church. Oh, what h_ _ _ she endured for that grand illusion!

Suddenly, my mental wanderings were interrupted by the blaring honks of several rude drivers—that's common to Atlanta drivers, too—and I realized my hands were not on the steering wheel, rather I was massaging my scalp from the memory. I arrived at the hair salon (the Atlanta term for beauty shop), and the stylist greeted me and walked me to his chair.

I was seated before wrap-around mirrors, and the stylist introduced me to his assistant, who would become my personal assistant during the appointment. After explaining that she would escort me to the different areas of the salon, be available to answer any questions, and create a portfolio of the various products used, she quietly and efficiently placed my purse in a lovely large bag. Yes, a bag for a bag. (At the end of the day when I paid the bill, I understood why purses receive special attention in an Atlanta hair salon!)

The experience—start to finish—was more than I expected. The stylist utilized his creative energy and innovative talent to produce an "ooh la la!" effect. The colorist meticulously highlighted strands to give the illusion of depth and volume to the style. I felt as if I had entered a sanctuary of luxury, but surprisingly everyone focused on service without pretentiousness. Each was an artist who had honed their craft.

At the payment desk, I did consider taking "the midnight train from Georgia," just to escape telling my husband the cost of my birthday treat.

I knew how blessed this Mexia girl was for having such a luxurious day! In a melancholy mood, though, I wished I could share the day with Mother. I wanted to tell her how many people it took to do her job, how sorry I was for being such a drama queen when she was doing her best, and how I longed to hear her say—"Gwen, your hair looks just beautiful." That would be the priceless present!

Gift Seven

Life Can Limit the Body but Never the Spirit

The last classes to attend Mexia Elementary School included 34 students in grades 1-4. Pictured are Miss Jewel Farish (last row, second from right) and (lst row, from right to left) Gwen Jaye (2nd student) Sherry Jaye (4th student), and Ginger Jaye (7th student).

Everything about her physical presence said, "Life can limit you." The steel braces that wrapped her legs, the deliberate way she swung her body to put one leg in front of the other, those metal poles she leaned on. I'd like to say that seeing her day after day at school, I grew accustomed to what the polio had done to her body.

But even a young child like me could see how much effort she put into every movement.

Miss Jewel Farish taught me in first, second, and third grade at Mexia School in the mid-1950s. Her workplace was a one-room rural school without indoor toilets, which meant she had to walk to the edge of the property to the outhouse several times a day. This was far from the only hurdle she faced: Miss Farish taught three grades in that room, and like other rural schools in Alabama at the time, nearly 43% of the students were living in poverty. Risk of academic failure was high, but as in everything else she attempted, she found a way forward.

Miss Farish had older third-grade students listen and instruct younger children in reading, writing, and arithmetic. She promoted reading and writing all day long. Without the aid of "ditto machines," which could leave your hands purple from the ink, she insisted that students write about their reading, draw scenes from the reading, and talk about it together as they gathered around the pot-bellied stove in the center of the room.

She created a sense of belonging by planning parent/teacher events for the town of Mexia at the schoolhouse. These even came in the form of square dances (never mind the fact that she could not physically participate). "Bow to your partner, bow to your corner, do si do," the caller would shout. Even the Baptists stepped into "Swing your partner, round and round," which, as many of us can remember, was a sight to behold in the 1950s.

Still, nowhere was this sense of community stronger than in her classroom. One bright, sunny day, we heard gunshots coming from the direction of Mexia Baptist Church cemetery. Despite Miss Farish's warning, we raced to the large-paned windows expecting to see a policeman or a hunter. What we saw instead was sad and sobering. Jimmy, a young, mentally challenged man we knew from the community, was sitting on the newly dug grave of his father sobbing. He ranted and fired rounds of bullets into the air. In a calm voice, Miss Farish told us to go to the coat closet. Then she summoned two of my older boy cousins. "Go to the grave and sit with Jimmy. Just listen to him talk for a while," she instructed. "Then ask him for his gun and tell him to come see me."

While I'm not advocating her approach to this situation in today's world, her response struck me then as it does now: full of kindness and mercy. And maybe, just maybe, she recalled a time when she herself had pleaded with God to give her a reason things are the way they are.

Miss Farish taught me for three years, she taught my sister Ginger for three years, and she taught my sister Sherry for one year at Mexia School—three Jaye girls in her classroom for six consecutive years. I have no doubt that the firm foundation Miss Farish gave us served us like a springboard to pursue our own careers in education. Combined, the three of us sisters have taught grades from kindergarten to doctorate-level classes.

Having taught generations of teachers, I see the wisdom Miss Farish practiced in her simple schoolroom in Mexia. More than sixty years later, many of her methods are cited as best practices in contemporary educational literature. For instance, the teacher/student relationships she forged among her older and younger pupils are overwhelmingly effective. Studies show that both the learner who is being tutored and the one who is doing the tutoring show significant gains in achievement (today, sadly, today most school systems separate students by academic ratings which can limit their achievement). Furthermore, literacy experts today insist that excessive worksheets limit critical thinking and active engagement. Her less structured approach to processing information is a much better tool for building literacy skills.

Her most valuable lesson, though, has less to do with *how* she taught, but rather, *what* she taught us. Though polio had limited her mobility, Miss Farish was propelled by an abundance of willpower, determination and grit. Her presence alone taught us a powerful life lesson: life can limit the body, but never the spirit.

When I received my doctor's degree in education, my sisters gave me a framed vintage picture card of Dick, Jane, and Spot from the primer book that Miss Farish used for instruction in our first grade classroom. I often look at it and think of Miss Farish, jewel of Mexia, standing tall.

School Fears—Simply Smile and Trust

During the summer of 1958, the upcoming consolidation of Mexia School into Monroeville Elementary School caused quite a stir among everyone in our small, rural community. The reasons for the consolidation were that a bigger school could provide a wider range of educational opportunities, and that closing Mexia School would save money within the county.

No matter whether you were attending a wedding or a funeral, you could not escape the constant chatter about this change and its implications to our community and to the students. The move was akin to moving Mayberry's jail to Mount Airy.

Every Sunday morning following the preacher's benediction, mothers would quickly gather on the front steps of the church to ponder this new edict from the board of education: *Will our children be academically prepared? How will they adjust to classroom sizes larger than the entire school of Mexia? Would the school shun the children? Will the students make new friends?*

As a nine-year-old child, I listened intently to the mothers' ponderings and internalized their concerns about attending a city school. *Was I smart enough to attend*

Monroeville Elementary? (Everyone seemed to think that a bigger school produced better students!) *Would I fit in at such a big school?* (I thought that being from the country wasn't so bad, but everyone made it sound hokey.) *Would I make new friends?* (In other words, would other students like a country bumpkin?) *Could I find my way around in such a large building?* (Mexia School only had two rooms). I worried and worried and worried.

This upcoming change reminded me of Aesop's fable of *The City Mouse and the Country Mouse.* I wondered if a country kid could adapt to a city school. As I thought about the tale, I wondered if there were frightening things in the town that could cause me harm.

The schoolhouse in Mexia was an integral part of community life. It was the place where Baptists, Methodists, Hard-Shell Baptists, and even non-churched people gathered for special programs, such as talent shows and square dancing.

Surely the city folks in Monroeville didn't know about the special things that made our school so worthy of our affection: If all 31 students had perfect attendance for a six-week reporting period, we walked to Mr. Brown's store for ice cream! We enjoyed plays and performances at the school where every student from first to fourth grade was a star. Mrs. Vinnie, the lunchroom worker, let us pull syrup until it became taffy candy.

Would there be things to love at a city school? Through my nine-year-old eyes, Monroeville was a metropolis.

So far in my young life, I loved everything about the first day of school—the smell of new books, chalk, and glue, and such. I made up my mind that no matter what, I was going to be ready for a great fifth-grade year at Monroeville Elementary. Still, anxiety lived alongside anticipation as a new school year approached.

To my pleasant surprise, my first day of school at Monroeville Elementary was absolutely wonderful. My teacher, Mrs. Cain, lovingly welcomed me and told the class about field trips, plays, and an upcoming end-of-the year event, the maypole dance. At recess, we had jungle gyms to climb and aluminum slides to race down. My thoughts were twirling as fast as the tilt-a-whirl on the playground imagining the new experiences ahead.

I just knew that I'd be a country girl who loved a city school, and unlike the country mouse there was nothing to fear about the city school…that was, until the bell rang for dismissal.

When Mrs. Cain asked for volunteers to help clean the room before we left for the day, my hand quickly shot into the air to help. Mrs. Cain asked me to beat the chalk erasers on the sidewalk. Busy pounding the felt onto the concrete, I heard the bell ring. Suddenly children were walking and running every-which-a-way, and I realized that I was on my own. Where should I go? Where are the buses? All the other children had quickly vanished like the chalk dust had in the air.

I scurried inside, grabbed my new book bag, and walked along the maze of sidewalks trying to find a familiar face. I was frightened, and my emotions were hanging on the slenderest of threads. I was lost. The maze of sidewalks seemed unending. Which way should I go?

At my lowest point, I heard a familiar voice. It was Mr. Thames, our bus driver from Mexia, calling my name. Like Samuel in the Bible, I quickly answered, "Here I am." He started leading me along the sidewalks toward the way to the bus, and I followed.

Mr. Thames never uttered a warning to me about not being at the loading zone, the way the other children knew to be. He never mentioned that our bus was the only one left in the parking lot when I stepped into the bus or shamed me for not knowing where to go. He just slowly put the bus into gear, and we left this place of new adventures and learning and moved back towards an old, familiar one.

Today, as a retired educator, I always especially feel for children, wherever they are from, who are about to embark on their first day of a school year. For example, in a few weeks, my grandchildren are transferring from one school into a new school district. Just as I once did, they are wondering and worrying about the move from one school to another. At bedtime, they've asked me: Do you think my reading, writing, and arithmetic will be as good as theirs will? Will I make new friends? How will I find the cafeteria?

At these common fears, I simply smile, trusting that they too will each find their own Mrs. Cain and Mr. Thames.

Mexia Elementary School

Gift Nine

A Teaching Legacy Shining Brightly

(Written upon learning of the death of Mrs. Sue Owens on December 16, 2017)

Photograph of my class with Miss Shumack. Gwen Jaye, standing far right. Miss Shumack, standing by tree.

Two students at a time entered the darkness of the janitor's closet on the sixth-grade hallway at Monroeville Elementary School. As the door closed, a beam of light from a flashlight shone on a basketball held by a classmate in the center of the dark, cavernous space. The two students watched as one of their classmates spun in the reflected light and as another student walked slowly around a traced path on the tiled floor.

Miss Shumack led this hands-on science activity to demonstrate rotation and revolution. Although this presentation happened almost 60 years ago, it was typical of ways Miss Shumack engaged 34 sixth-grade students in learning. Students were actively doing science, not just listening or reading about science.

Such is the teaching legacy of Miss Shumack.

Miss Shumack was a young first-year teacher when I was her pupil in the sixth grade. As an educator for many years, I still remember my first year of teaching. There are so many fears—imagined and real—to face. Teaching is a career filled with numerous joys, but it is not one without worries or profound consequences. Miss Shumack needed not to worry at all. The key ingredient for her success could be embodied in one word: care.

Often students express their emotions about a favorite teacher by saying, "I love my teacher." There are many emotions in this simple, childlike phrase. If a teacher cares, she/he will provide appropriate instruction, will create activities that promote the good of each person, and will model behaviors students will emulate.

Miss Shumack provided appropriate instruction for learners in her classroom. Not only did she give individual and independent assignments, she promoted cooperative group work. While other students may recall other key moments of joy in her classroom, I remember studying the states with one such group.

Mary Elaine Jackson, Allen Dunning, George Duncan and I were assigned to present information on North Carolina. Our research included learning about the capital city, products made there, the history of the state, and famous people from the state. Miss Shumack incorporated music and movement with reading and writing to make the study meaningful. So our group performed *Carolina Moon Keep Shining,* with Miss Shumack directing.

Miss Shumack initiated the Maypole Dance as the end-of-the-school-year activity. Girls and boys laced colorful ribbons around the Maypole anchored in the front of the school. Girls wore shirts of every color found in a crayon box—fancy pink, pastel blue, Easter green, sunlight yellow—and the boys wore their best pants and shirts. What a beautiful scene we were, weaving in and out, crisscrossing our streamers! This memory never fades.

Ginger, my sister, had Miss Shumack for sixth grade the next year. I'm certain that mother and daddy were so pleased with my experiences that they requested Ginger's placement in her classroom. Miss Shumack got married that year. Ginger remembers that the hardest thing about sixth grade was learning to say Mrs. Owens instead of Miss Shumack. Mother took us to Monroeville to buy a wedding gift, and we gave it to the new bride with great pride. Of course, Mrs. Owens said it was her favorite gift.

Years later when I would come to Mexia for a visit, I often saw Mrs. Owens. I would embrace her and tell her my favorite memory of my sixth-grade year, and she would listen with all the grace I expected from such a loving person. Here is the story to which she listened *too, too, too* many times:

Our class had moved from the study of the history of the United States to learning about the continent of South America. Even today, I can rattle off the countries and major cities of this land region, due to Miss Shumack's teaching techniques. She let us explore the continent in various ways, but the one that I will forever remember is going to the Port of Mobile to see a ship from Brazil enter the port. We watched as workers unloaded bananas from the largest vessel I had ever seen.

This field trip broadened my real-life knowledge of the world. I learned about the culture and products from other countries, our state's industry, the importance of waterways, etc. When I became an educator, I incorporated field trips into units of study with students from first grade to college level because of the lasting impact of this experience.

After returning from the field trip (I wore my fanciest dress to impress Miss Shumack), she drove me home, because Mother and Daddy were in Texas attending a convention. This brief uninterrupted time with my teacher was extra special to me. In the car, I talked without taking a breath (she confirmed this fact) about how much I appreciated the trip. I even told her that whenever I ate a banana, I'd remember that trip, and her. And I do, even to this day.

Recently, Mrs. Owens wrote a note to me about my writings that were published in *The Monroe Journal.* I treasure her words of affirmation, kindness, and love.

Teaching is not so much about what you teach, but how you teach. Miss Shumack knew this lesson well. She shines on in the hearts of those fortunate enough to have called her "my teacher."

Gift Ten

Crazy Bad Things Can Be Crazy Good

Robert Earl Thompson

As a child at Mexia Baptist Church, it was sometimes difficult to distinguish between what was crazy bad and crazy good in religion.

Often a revival minister, and sometimes the ministers of the church, asked the congregation to sing ALL SIX stanzas of *Just as I Am*—twice! Crazy bad!

My octogenarian great-uncle, Ruben Jay, the oldest church member when I was a pre-teen, was beloved by the congregation—despite his outrageously l-e-n-g-t-h-y prayers. If he prayed at the end of a Sunday night service, the latest episode of the adventures of Ben Cartwright and his sons would start and end before his "Amen."

The congregation's vexation about the length of Uncle Rube's public prayers became torment at one annual Mexia Baptist Church homecoming, which was the *crème de la crème* in good singing, good preaching, and GOOD FOOD.

The guest minister asked Uncle Rube to say grace before the homecoming meal. Sounding like a host of archangels, this patriarchal father of the church asked the congregation to join him in fervent and holy prayer.

Who, may I ask, would want to wait a minute to eat when fresh butterbeans and peas, fried okra, Mrs. Opal's famous corn pudding, Marion's chicken and dumplings, Myrtle's banana pudding, and Mrs. Sarah's pound cake as well as other homemade delicacies from the best cooks ever assembled under one church roof were ready in the fellowship hall? (A sensible prayer for this situation would have been the child's prayer, "God is great, God is good, let us thank Him for our food"!)

But we had to wait a long time for the prepared banquet...Crazy bad!

Occasionally, on Sunday evenings we sang the Jubilee Song, *Give Me That Old Time Religion.* After singing the familiar lyrics—"It was good for the Hebrew children and It was good for Paul and Silas"—the song leader, Junior Nettles, asked members to supply names of ancestors and/or church leaders to place in the stanzas.

A name frequently inserted was that of Uncle Rube of l-e-n-g-t-h-y prayer fame.

Uncle Rube

Fifty years later, the significance of Uncle Rube's name inserted in a stanza of *Give Me that Old Time Religion* became real for me…

For almost twenty-five years, I taught an adult Sunday school class at Vestavia Hills Baptist Church in Birmingham, a church full of wonderful people, situated on a bluff of Shades Mountain that overlooks the beautiful vistas of Birmingham, and surrounded by neighborhoods full of opulent homes. Often, the introduction to the lesson began with what the class members affectionately called a "Mexia Story."

At the end of the lesson one Sunday, I asked a visiting couple to introduce themselves to the class. The guest said he was from Mexia. His name was Robert Earl Thompson, brother to Susan Williams of Mexia, organist for Mexia Baptist Church for over 50 years, and whose family were founding members of the church.

Robert Earl asked me if he could give a follow-up "Mexia Story" that connected to the lesson theme on giving joyfully to the Lord. He began by stating that during the difficult days of the Great Depression, Uncle Rube and my grandfather, Thomas Herndon Jay, pooled their money to buy a New Testament for each of the senior class graduates from Mexia Baptist Church. Robert Earl was one of the recipients, and he told with details and with deep affection about the significance of that gift in his life.

Afterwards, I pondered the mysteries of faith embedded in his inspiring conclusion to the lesson. Every statistic about Alabama farmers and the harsh economic conditions they faced during the Great

Depression would lead you to question the sanity of not one, but two, farmers spending at least a week's wages on buying Bibles for high school graduates. But it was crazy good, right?

How amazing that the names of two poor South Alabama Christians who sacrificially gave to others would be praised in one of the most affluent churches in Alabama. Unbelievably crazy!

Give Me That Old Time Religion refers to stories of faith and courage and love from ancestors of the past. However, the teachings of Mexia Baptist Church often live in service today. The following true story is like that of the biblical book of Samuel.

Several years ago, my sister and her husband, Ginger and David Smith, moved from Richmond, Virginia, to an unincorporated area on Lake Wateree in Ridgeway, South Carolina. Moving from a large city with unlimited access to shopping, restaurants, and entertainment venues to a lakeside community that requires at least a 15-minute drive to even a grocery store has been limiting and challenging for them.

Like Little Red Hen in the children's storybook, Ginger's life in Richmond had been busy! Her life was crammed with a hectic work schedule at Children's Hospital, civic responsibilities in her neighborhood, and Sunday responsibilities at First Baptist Church of

Richmond, whose motto is "Bringing the Kingdom of God to the people of Richmond."

With the move, Ginger's hectic schedule suddenly stopped in its tracks. With time to spare, Ginger thought more about the motto of her church and considered her responsibility in "Bringing the Kingdom of God to the people in Ridgeway, South Carolina."

On her way to her new church, Ginger passed Ridgeway Manor, a nursing facility that sat isolated and lonely, off the road in a field of grass. As Ginger tells it, she heard a voice speak to her that said, "This is the place." She replied, "Not there. I don't connect to elderly people or the sick, and I'm certainly hate the smell often found there. Give me people who can think deeply about Scripture, and who can challenge my thoughts."

On her next trip past the facility, the voice came again. She audibly repeated her objections more forcibly this time. The third time the voice sounded, Ginger acquiesced and called the administration about ways to help the residents.

Well, the rest of the story is CRAZY GOOD! Ginger is beginning her fourth year of teaching a Bible study class to the residents there who are poor in mind, body, and/or spirit. But she does so much more. She loves the people and finds numerous ways to meet their needs. Somehow, Ginger forgets the smells, too.

Can Bible Scriptures taught long ago at Mexia Baptist Church find their way into today's world with relevance?

Ask the residents of this Ridgeway, South Carolina, nursing home who are ministered to physical, emotionally, and spiritually every Wednesday by a woman with Mexia Baptist Church roots, and you'll hear: It's CRAZY GOOD!

That's the thing about good religion—crazy things, even crazy bad things, *can be* crazy good.

However, I will never be convinced that singing more than three stanzas of *Just as I Am* is crazy good!

A Mission Lesson in Memphis

Mexia Baptist Church

In the spring of 1963, George Wallace's "Stand in the Schoolhouse Door" and the violence in the streets of Birmingham seemed far removed from the here and now of my mundane life as an egocentric fourteen-year-old girl living in Mexia. While newsreels on the CBS Evening News with Walter Cronkite showed seismic scenes of injustice and inequality in Alabama, a placid status quo permeated my world, that was, until I attended a mission convention in Memphis.

Mexia Baptist Church and missions were like peas and cornbread—they just went together. Not only did Mexia Baptist churchgoers believe in missions, they practiced their beliefs by providing mission education, by giving financial support to the Southern Baptist Convention mission efforts, and by encouraging mission work at home and around the globe.

Girls and boys who enrolled in the missions education groups—Sunbeams, GAs (Girls' Auxiliary) and RAs (Royal Ambassadors)—at Mexia Baptist learned more about continents, countries, and foreign and national cities from mission study than they did from the public school curriculum.

On Wednesday nights at Prayer Meeting, names of missionaries who had birthdays that week were read aloud, and prayers of blessings for their work and for their safekeeping floated heavenward. When missionaries Tom and Gloria Thurman (Bethlehem Baptist Association missionaries who were appointed to Asia) and Bob and Mavis Shivers Hardy (missionaries to Japan born in Frisco City) came home on furlough, they received a welcome as gracious as the one given to the Prodigal Son.

When Mrs. B. F. Chambers, a resident of Frisco City who served as head of the WMU for the Bethlehem Baptist Association, invited my sister, Ginger, and me to attend the Girls' Auxiliary 50th Anniversary Convention in Memphis, it was as if "Heaven Came Down" right there in Mexia for us.

Ginger and I were aware that our parents' decision could hinge on whether we would be safe amid the protests, sit-ins, and marches gaining momentum in Southern cities. However, Christian mission growth opportunities outweighed their reluctance over these issues. Ginger and I were filled with the same anticipation for the trip that one has on Christmas Eve for Christmas Day. At precisely eight o'clock in the morning on June 17, 1963, Mrs. Chambers drove into our driveway in her new lipstick-red Cadillac—our magic carpet ride to glory!

In Memphis, when we entered Ellis Auditorium on Tuesday evening at seven o'clock with over 7,000 other girls, we stepped into a world of nations. Missionaries from every continent informed us about their work, authors of our GA materials proclaimed the "Good News," and girl voices sang in harmony so loudly that surely the mighty Mississippi River clapped for joy, echoing King David's delight in worship.

On the last day of the convention, our group walked to Woolworth's for lunch. As we filed into the lunch counter with other customers, a group of young black men, so impeccably dressed that we seemed out of place in new convention clothes, followed behind us. Our group took a seat at a round table that accommodated four wrought-iron chairs, and the men sat at the gleaming white marble lunch counter.

After we had received our hamburger and fries, I noticed that the waitress was ignoring all signs from the black men that they were ready to order. I anxiously scrutinized the exchange between the two. She refused to look their way and even turned her body away from the group.

Mrs. Chambers must have noticed my rapt attention to the ongoing situation for she asked me to not to stare. However, how could I not? While aware that sit-in protests occurred, I was totally unprepared for the blatant shunning taking place. Surely others noticed and would react! However, like the waitress, they all ignored the group.

Glued to my chair, I thought about the worship services we had just attended. Were the themes of the messages "A Message to Give to the Nations," and "A Savior to Show to the Nations" made for a situation such as this? Would missionaries from Ghana, Nigeria, Jamaica and the San Blas Islands have sprung into action? Would the speakers have refused to eat their meal to show support for the young men? Would convention-goers have left in protest? What was a white, Christian girl who had just listened about a Savior's love for all to do in this situation?

My thoughts were abruptly ended as policemen swung open the double doors to the building. A queasy feeling churned in the pit of my stomach. Their presence was menacing, and it saturated the restaurant like a putrid odor.

With a sauntering walk that spoke of presupposed prejudices, the officers pointed the ends of bully-sticks toward the men. What could happen? As if in slow motion, the group of men came to their feet, looked the policemen in the eyes and then surveyed the people in the room. The scene created a silence that was screaming for a response. Not a word, not a movement, not a hand of grace.

Like the others, I turned my eyes to the table, avoiding what I imagined as a plea for action and mercy. The Spirit penetrated my heart and I knew I was like the Pharisee who crossed to the other side of the road.

Everyone watched as the men left the eatery, as quietly as they had sat waiting for their food. Watching with a heavy heart, I thought there was a noticeable gracefulness in the groups' stride as they exited the building that said, "We Shall Overcome."

I created an altered vision for myself that day, and in that new mirage I followed the group of young men out onto the streets of Memphis. What would have happened if a white, fourteen-year-old girl had stepped outside with them?

I often wonder.

Gift Twelve

A Song in the Air at Mexia

Mexia Baptist Church Choir

The longing for home swept over me at Christmas time in 2017. As C. S. Lewis explains, longing for home often refers to memories of how life was at a point in time—all the sights, sounds, feelings, and emotions of a place.

During my childhood, an essential part of Mexia and Mexia Baptist Church was music. Just as works and faith live together, so did Mexia and music. The memories of Mexia and music unfolded as I drove to attend the Christmas cantata at Mexia Baptist Church.

My earliest memories of members of the Mexia community meeting together are at homecoming dinners on the ground and at community singings in various homes. Someone asked me recently, "What did you do at singings?" The reply was simple, "Sing."

It only took one phone call to contact at least nine people about the time and day of the singing, because Mexia was part of the "party line" telephone system. (You could always count on someone listening in on your phone conversation.)

Junior Nettles began the evening event by passing around Stamp Baxter songbooks as Aunt Rachel made her way through the crowd to her throne (piano bench).

Decorum demanded that she ask if anyone else wanted to play—they knew that even if Jerry Lee Lewis appeared, he would not be sitting on that piano bench.

Aunt Rachel was the only one in the crowd without a songbook. It almost defied logic, but she never learned to read music. Not only did Aunt Rachel know every note to play, she also knew what song occupied page 15 or 115 or 200.

After surveying the keys as general might inspect his troops, Aunt Rachel gave a grand fanfare prelude that solidified her position as the reigning pianist. This commanding performance was followed a slight turn of her head to Junior to signal that singing could commence.

The first songs of the evening were for everyone to sing and included favorite selections like *Just a Little Talk with Jesus.* After refreshments, the songs of the second half focused on hearing the solo voices of Woodrow Jaye, bass; Kenneth Johnson, tenor; or Mary Jaye Green, soprano or alto—depending on whether Junior took the lead in songs like *Golden Jubilee,* or *I Bowed On My Knees and Cried Holy,* or *I'll Meet You By the River.*

The crowd always demanded an encore, and this is when Aunt Rachel would really shine. Her posture on the piano stool indicated serious business, and the only words to describe what followed next is, "She took off!"

With fingers dancing on and off white and black keys, she played lightning-fast scales and arpeggios and you would swear that you could hear piccolos, flutes, oboes, saxophones, drums, trumpets—all the instruments of a big marching band as she played *Under the Double Eagle* composed by Josef Franz Wagner, the March King of Austria.

(I doubt that anyone knew that Aunt Rachel was enriching all of our lives by playing classical music. Oh, the things you can learn by attending a singing.)

No one in Mexia ever preached that music is transformative in improving health, mentally and physically; that music aids in improving children's vocabulary development, fluency, and comprehension reading skills; and, that music helps in healing after a loss. Rather, these benefits were just naturally accepted.

We understood that music was good for the young and old alike, and that you needed music just as you needed food and drink. Music and Mexia were a duet.

Mexia Baptist Church marked new Sunday school classes by grade levels. However, significant birthdays were celebrated by moving from the children's choir to youth choir to adult choir.

Names ending in Thompson, Nettles, Johnson, and Jaye appeared regularly in church bulletins under the heading, "Special Music." For over a century, members of these families played the piano, conducted choirs, and/or led the music.

Today, Susan Thompson Williams plays the organ and Martha Johnson Payne (her mother was a Jaye) plays the piano. Martha only had three piano lessons in her life—I kid and tell her that she must have had a supernatural teacher.

As I entered the sanctuary on a cold, rainy December night, these memories occupied my mind. Several of my cousins had invited me to attend the cantata because they were proud of the growth of the choir musically under the direction of Terry Barksdale, a Samford University graduate with a specialization in conducting.

The performance of the choir exceeded my cousins' praises. The choir members blended in a balanced manner and the intonation, diction, and rhythm combined to create an excellent musical performance. Mr. Barksdale shaped the words and music beautifully, and the choir followed him like the Bremen Town Musicians.

There were many highlights of the evening, like the heartfelt solo by Larry Burt, former choir director.

However, no highlight was more beautiful than seeing and hearing the children of Mexia sing with confidence, ability, and joy. It was enough to make the heart sing.

How wonderful it is to know that a bright future lies ahead for the choir. It was evident that strengths of the past—commitment, punctuality, prayer, attentiveness—remain. But much more has been added.

Other names will continue to bless the music coming from Mexia, for the church is a living place, and because there's just a song in the air in Mexia.

Mexia and music go together. Isn't it wonderful to be defined by singing?

What the world needs now is a song to sing. Sing glad tidings, Mexia Baptist Choir!

Martha Payne, pianist, and Susan Thompson Williams, organist, of Mexia Baptist Church.

Beauty Extends Beyond the Surface

Summertime in Mexia was for putting up vegetables. Right up until the day my mother asked a pair of Manhattan fashion models to put on a runway show in the living room of our 1950s ranch house, it's almost all we did. Mother was a big believer that children should grow up outdoors (and firmly against child labor laws), and Daddy had one of the most prolific gardens in the county. So, during canning season, my sisters and I spent most of our days shelling butter beans and peas, cutting okra, and shucking corn on the carport or under a tree in the yard.

I remember looking out at US Highway 84 in front of our house and dreaming of following its black pavement to other places. Exciting places.

But the only work release Mother granted during those summers was a two-hour reprieve for reading. It was required, but it didn't have to be. I loved those hours—not just because it was the only time between 7:30 and 5:00 that I could actually go inside, but because reading let me travel far beyond the bounds of the cotton fields and farmland of Mexia. *Nancy Drew, The Hardy Boys, Trixie Belden,* any biography on a First Lady—these stories let me paint a canvas in my mind that was filled with discovery and friendship, love and redemption, and so much more.

Mother often told my sisters and me that we could find those same universal themes in the real-life experiences of the people in our rural, isolated community. I'm not sure I believed her. How could rousing stories spring from people who farmed cotton and corn, and who attended Mexia Baptist Church at least three times every week?

Surely their lives were as ordinary and mundane as I thought mine to be.

But the truth of Mother's comments did eventually take root. One day, she simply announced that a pair of famous fashion models had agreed to give a runway show of the latest styles in our living room. The Ward sisters, she called them.

Even as Mother explained that their father lived in Mexia, which was the reason for their visit, my sisters and I were full of questions. Why would these seemingly wealthy, sophisticated models agree to do this, and who was this 'Mr. Ward?' We'd never heard of him.

"He's a Methodist," Mother told us.

That explained it. There were only two groups of people in Mexia—the Baptists and the Methodists, and we only knew the former.

Mother didn't have time for the rest of our questions; there was work to be done. For the first time I could remember, garden chores took a back seat. My sister Sherry and I transformed our bedroom into a dressing room and cleared our closet to use as a wardrobe rack. We cut the crust away from countless slices of bread for tea sandwiches and we pushed all the furniture in the living and dining rooms against the wall to make way for the runway (I thought the chairs and sofa lined up just so looked like silent soldiers standing guard over our big event).

On the day of the show, ladies from Mexia Baptist Church filled the house. Background music played as Mother emceed the fashion show. Oohs and ahhs erupted from the guests as the sisters emerged from the bedroom in their finery. (Our suspicions that the sisters were wealthy were confirmed when Sherry told us that she spotted lace bras on the bed. Lace!)

Amid all the excitement and wonder of the models' visit to our house, there were also hushed conversations around the punch bowl about just how wealthy the sisters were, and about the fact that one had married a Jewish man. My young mind was spinning faster than the ladle mixing the sherbet in the bowl—was being wealthy a sin? Can one be wealthy and serve God? I knew the parable of the rich man, but I also knew that God loved King David, who had to be wealthy. Gosh, Jews didn't believe in Jesus. Should we tell the Gospel story or remain quiet?

To me, an eternal heaven and hell story was playing out right there in our living room.

The memories of that day have dimmed through the years. My sisters and I might have even forgotten about it had it not been for a recent correspondence with Mr. George Jones. He sent me a story he had written for *The Monroe Journal* several years before, titled *Mexia's Ward Sisters Captivated New York.*

His story confirmed that truth can be more interesting than one can imagine. Here are just some of the highlights from his story: The older of the two, Kitty, modeled for the Powers Modeling Agency, which led to a fashion position in Paris. She and her husband went on to build one of the world's largest manufacturers of children's clothing in the world. As for the younger, Doris, she worked for Barbizon Modeling Agency, which also carried her around the world. She married a decorated war hero and diplomat in the Foreign Service, and settled on 500-acre plantation in St. Thomas.

I've often wondered how this small-town fashion show and tea would be told from the Ward sisters' point of view? What did they think of walking down that runway in a 1950s ranch in rural Alabama? Were we just country bumpkins to them or were they just as gracious as I remember?

I never saw them again after that day, but I do have a clue on their good character.

About 30 years later, my beloved Aunt Nona married Mr. Ward, the Methodist. Both were in their late 70s and had lived in Mexia all their lives. I doubt if either had traveled further than a couple hundred miles from home. So it was especially heartwarming to hear that the Ward sisters sent the septuagenarian newlyweds on a honeymoon to the Bahamas and New York City. I think even the best fairy tales have trouble matching that ending!

Interesting stories indeed came out of our own backyard. The day the Ward sisters came to Mexia, universal truths connected us all. Beauty often extends well beyond what we could see on the surface. The power of community can be magnetic (no matter how far you roam). Religious divides aren't as big as they appear. Love is ageless.

And of course, Mother was right, which is perhaps the most enduring lesson of them all!

Gift Fourteen

Uncle Click's Normandy Memories

Mr. Jaye (l) and Uncle Click (r)

In August of this year, my husband and I went to Normandy, France to tour the Normandy beaches. We especially wanted to see Omaha Beach, where my uncle, Royden Ellis (Click) Jaye came ashore as a special reconnaissance officer on the second wave of the Allied invasion on D-Day, June 6, 1944. Uncle Click was part of a special unit of men who climbed those famous cliffs and set the course for victory for the Allies on the Western front. However, he never talked about his experiences. Providentially, my trip prompted Uncle Click to share with the family his memories of landing with Operation Overlord.

At three different times in early 1942, my grandparents stood solemnly on their front porch and watched one of their sons walk away from the home place to a distant war. This scene was not like my childhood images; there were no people gathering with bands to cheer on the soldiers. There were no banners or bugles blaring, only heartache, watching, and walking. In typical stoic fashion and with undying faith, Granddaddy returned to the fields, Grandmother returned to the kitchen, and younger children returned to play after each son left.

During the past 60-plus years, my generation (those born after the war) learned only snippets of information from aunts and older cousins—who were young children at the time—about my father and uncles' service to our country. At countless family gatherings and patriotic community events during the years, my father and uncles' personal voices about the war remained silent—years that had made such a significant difference in their lives. We were the baby boomers, yet World War II was light years away.

My father, David Bartley Jaye, served in the war in England, but facts, battles, and/or stories related to his service were left to our imaginations. In our imaginations, we made his life before our births one of childhood folkloric themes: bravery, love, and sacrifice. How brave it was for Daddy to go to Monroeville and enlist in a war that would take him away from all he knew! His dog Monk refused to eat or drink after he left, which became a metaphor of love. Granddaddy Jaye had a place in the woods where he prayed every day for his sons. The ground was worn bare from his fervent prayers. Then, after five years of war, Daddy unexpectedly and nonchalantly arrived home in the middle of the night by taxi.

It was only during the last weeks of his 91 years that Daddy talked about his service with the 351st Bomb Group of the 8th Air Corps Division in England. He told us that his life at that point was truly the worst of times, but also the best of times. Perhaps older and wiser, we understood that Daddy was continuing to give us life lessons in his last days. We learned from him that in times of hardship and trial, character is produced; that promises made to the Lord require commitment; and mostly, that life is to be valued.

Through hushed conversations, my sisters and I also learned that Uncle Click returned home reliving horrific events from the war. He would erupt in nightmarish screams and emotional outbursts, trigged by common everyday sounds such as a neighbor's shotgun blast while squirrel hunting. It is told that Uncle Click gave his shotgun to his nephew after the war, and after his return he never again enjoyed the woods, or hunting with his brothers.

When my husband and I returned home from France, the family celebrated Uncle Click's 95th birthday. At the party, I laid out a map of Normandy on the table, and he began to trace his steps across the map. He talked about towns and battles that were part of the D-Day offensive and the 100-day offensive which turned the tide for the region and the world. "In Caen," he added, "we endured such fierce fighting that the town was destroyed. Rouen," he continued, "was where the German 7th Army gave up after three months of fierce fighting." After talking about the long-fought battle for Normandy, he marked out his route from France to Belgium, Luxembourg, Germany, Austria, and Czechoslovakia with Patton's III Army, while shaking his head side to side, as if to brush away haunting scenes.

As a special reconnaissance officer that trained with the Rangers, he was one of seven soldiers sent on enemy patrols to scout the terrain, detect the enemy and infiltrate or raid the lines on June 7, 1944. He was the only one to return.

Pointing to Sainte-Mère-Église, he told how the Germans held French women of the village hostages as human shields in the church tower and made them shoot as soldiers approached the building. This cathedral was made famous in the film, *The Longest Day*.

"Do the French today even know we were there?" he asked. Despite my reassurances that not only do they know, the French have erected monuments and statues, and offer tours to document the sacrifices of American soldiers, I knew these recollections of memories would barely scratch the surface of the experiences he endured there.

As I was leaving the birthday party, I asked, "Did you and Daddy ever meet during the war?" "Yes, one time," he replied. Joyously, I exclaimed, "Well, I know there were hugs and brotherly slaps, and more hugs." To which he solemnly replied, "Well, you'd be whistling Dixie." "What?" I asked. "Well, there were no hugs," he stated. Astonished, I asked, "Well, what did you do and say to each other?" Softly, he replied, "We looked at each other, shook hands, asked 'How are you?' and then started talking about home."

The cost of our trip to Normandy, France, was pricey. The memories of being on that hallowed ground and then being with Uncle Click as he shared memories—PRICELESS! The time together was a time to honor my family's legacy to the big picture of our beloved county. Perhaps my experiences will inspire you to video, record, or write about your family's history of *The Greatest Generation* or of another family veteran. Their experiences deserve to be honored. You and many others will be blessed by their heritage of sacrifice to our nation.

Window in Mexia Baptist Church given in memory and honor of my grandparents, Thomas Herndon Jay and Ida Ann Jay.

Gift Fifteen

Gardens Remembered

In early spring, Daddy lined up nickel-paper bags holding just a sprinkling of butterbeans, peas, okra, and watermelon seeds on the long wooden table on the carport. It never ceased to amaze me that tiny seeds in small seed-bags would produce an extravagant abundance of crops for our family.

Before the seeds could be planted, Daddy had to wait for Bill and his mule, Nellie, to come plow the field. My sisters and I anticipated the duo's arrival, for there was something beautiful about how Bill and Nellie worked in tandem, tilling the rows. Bill uttered one-syllable commands to his mule, and the stubborn animal obeyed every "Gee" and "Haw" and "Whoa." A duet was being sung.

A couple of weeks after the seeds had been placed in the rich fertile soil, Daddy began a routine of hoeing, watering, and fertilizing the plants. His labor yielded a vegetable garden that should have made his head swell with pride to the size of a watermelon.

To my sisters' and my dismay, every year over and over again the beans, tomatoes, corn, and peas ripened on July 4. We spent this national holiday on the carport or under a tree shelling butterbeans and cutting corn as we dreamed of splashing in the cool ocean waters of Gulf Shores. We dared not complain because the 11th commandment at our house was, "Thou shall work before play."

Although I was thankful for the food gathered from the garden, I longed for a grand garden like the one in Frances Hodgson Burnett's classic children's book *The Secret Garden*—a garden where jasmine, rose, and gardenia fragrances filled the air and where grand stone statuary figures and fountains dotted the landscape.

Grandmother Jaye's yard was the closest thing to the author's description. Grandmother had flowers bunched together in patches that were as aesthetically appealing as the patterns she sewed in her quilts. Sitting in the swing on her front porch, which had wisteria vines clinging to the sides, it was easy to be lulled into thinking you were in the garden Colin and Mary found so enchanting.

Childhood experiences and memories of Daddy and Grandmother Jaye's gardens have led me to pursue gardening interests that have lain dormant for many years. So I said yes when asked to join the Marion Garden Club. My husband and I have joked that the reason we were asked to become members of this nonagenarian club is that we are young(er) and still fit enough to dig a hole for civic projects.

We are certainly novice gardeners—between us we can only name one or two annual or perennial plants. And weren't members mispronouncing *moles* when they said *voles?* Prior knowledge in the field of education kicked in, for didn't "round up" refer to getting children in lines?

After only a one-year membership with instruction in which plants attract birds and butterflies, which deter deer, and what are the differences between moles and voles, the group asked me to assume the role of vice president for a two-year period.

My lack of knowledge about gardening didn't faze me in accepting the role. As vice president, I would be creating program topics and a yearbook. These duties were simple enough for one accustomed to assigning research papers and for one who had published a gazillion educational booklets.

However, I failed to read the fine print of my duties, which included assuming the role of president of the club if the current president could not perform their role. Our president became seriously ill just prior to the Alabama District IV Fall Meeting, which the Marion Garden Club was hosting at Judson College. I had to take up her duties.

A district meeting is the "Big Kahuna"—attended by serious gardeners who are well versed in horticultural topics and who can identify every species of camellia grown in Alabama soil. To make matters worse, the president of the Garden Club of Alabama would be attending the meeting with other state officers. "Lordy, Lordy, Lordy," I said to myself.

The day of the meeting arrived. Food was prepared, tables set, guests welcomed, the Pledge of Allegiance recited, and suddenly it was my turn at the podium. I knew I couldn't bamboozle this group with gardening information, so I relied on memories of gardens from my childhood. After welcoming the group, I called attention to the Gladiolus flower arrangement on the table by the podium. I stated that this flower signifies remembrance, and I that I would like to share memories of two flowers with the group. So I began…

Sitting by my bed are two of my favorite family photographs of Grandfather Jaye and Grandmother Jaye in 1943. They sent the pictures to my father while he was stationed in Europe during World War II.

The snapshot of Granddaddy, who stood well over six feet tall, shows him in his cotton field with cotton bolls up to his shoulders. He wanted Daddy to know it had been a banner year.

Not to be outdone, Grandmother, a petite woman who stood less than 5 feet tall, was photographed standing in the midst of her sunflower garden with golden blooms up to her eyes.

Grandmother and Granddaddy Jaye sent reassuring words in a letter with the photographs that said, "The Maker of All was good to us."

After my remarks to the gardeners, I told the group that I was wearing Grandmother's pink shawl, which was given to me after her death.

I shared that I had never worn the shawl before, but that I was wearing it as a symbol of a family who had fed so many with nourishing food from the land around them, and who appreciated the bounty of the earth.

As I left the podium, applause filled the room. I knew within my heart that it was praise for a family who loved the beauty of the earth and took care of it. It was recognition for a family who knew that beauty and hard work often live alongside each other. And it was a family who knew the One who began the world in a garden.

www.ingramcontent.com/pod-product-compliance
Lightning Source LLC
Chambersburg PA
CBHW070449170726
48291CB00005B/1672

* 9 7 8 1 9 4 9 8 8 8 1 0 2 *